My Really Wheely RACING DAY!

Betty G. Birney worked at Disneyland and the Disney Studios, has written many children's television shows and is the author of over forty books, including the bestselling *The World According to Humphrey*, which won the Richard and Judy Children's Book Club Award, *Friendship According to Humphrey*, *Trouble According to Humphrey*, *Surprises According to Humphrey*, *More Adventures According to Humphrey*, *Holidays According to Humphrey*, *School According to Humphrey*, *Mysteries According to Humphrey* and *Christmas According to Humphrey*. This is the seventh book in her Humphrey's Tiny Tales series. Her work has won many awards, including an Emmy and three Humanitas Prizes. She lives in America with her husband.

60000237897

Have you read all of Humphrey's adventures?
The World According to Humphrey
Friendship According to Humphrey
Trouble According to Humphrey
Adventure According to Humphrey
(special publication for World Book Day 2008)
Surprises According to Humphrey
More Adventures According to Humphrey
Holidays According to Humphrey
School According to Humphrey
Mysteries According to Humphrey
Christmas According to Humphrey

Humphrey's Big-Big-Big Book of Stories (3 books in 1)
Humphrey's Great-Great-Great Book of Stories (3 books in 1)

Humphrey's Book of Fun-Fun-Fun
Humphrey's Ha-Ha-Ha Joke Book
Humphrey's World of Pets

Humphrey's Tiny Tales
My Pet Show Panic!
My Treasure Hunt Trouble!
My Summer Fair Surprise!
My Creepy-Crawly Camping Adventure!
My Great Big Birthday Bash!
My Playful Puppy Problem!

By the same author
The Princess and the Peabodys

Humphrey's Tiny Tales

My Really Wheely RACING DAY!

BETTY G. BIRNEY

Illustrated by Penny Dann

faber and faber

First published in 2013
by Faber and Faber Limited
Bloomsbury House, 74–77
Great Russell Street, London WC1B 3DA

Printed and bound by CPI Group (UK) Ltd, Croydon, CR0 4YY

A CIP record for this book
is available from the British Library

ISBN 978–0–571–29897–6

2 4 6 8 10 9 7 5 3 1

Welcome to MY WORLD

Hi! I'm Humphrey. I'm lucky to be the classroom hamster in Room 26 of Longfellow School. It's a big job because I have to go home with a different student each weekend and try to help my friends. Luckily, my cage has a lock-that-doesn't-lock, so I can get out and have BIG-BIG-BIG adventures!

I'd like you to meet some of my friends

Og

a frog, is the other classroom pet in Room 26. He makes a funny sound: BOING!

Aldo Amato

is a grownup who cleans Room 26 at night. He's a special friend who always brings me a treat and seems to understand my squeaks better than most humans.

Mrs Brisbane

is our teacher. She really understands her students – even me!

Mr Morales

is the head and the Most Important Person at Longfellow School.

Lower-Your-Voice-AJ

has a loud voice and calls me
Humphrey-Dumpty.

Golden-Miranda

has golden hair, like I do. She also
has a dog named Clem. Eeek!

Don't-Complain-Mandy

has a hamster named Winky!

Winky

is Mandy's pet hamster and one
of my favourite pals!

I think you'll like my other friends, too, such as
Wait-for-the-Bell-Garth, *Speak-Up-Sayeh*,
Stop-Giggling-Gail and *Pay-Attention-Art*.

CONTENTS

1 A Wheely Great Weekend   1

2 ZOOM-ZOOM-ZOOM
Around the Room   19

3 Really Wheely and Red   34

4 A Wheely Big Day   52

A Wheely Great Weekend

It was Friday afternoon in Room 26 of Longfellow School, and I was spinning on my hamster wheel, trying to stay calm.

Fridays are always exciting ... especially for me.

Every Friday afternoon, I get to go home with a different classmate.

It's the BEST-BEST-BEST part of

my job as classroom pet.

Of course, Mrs Brisbane already knew whose turn it was, because she plans my visits with the parents.

But sometimes she forgets to tell *me*.

Who would it be this week?

Would it be Lower-Your-Voice-AJ, whose whole family likes to talk?

Or would I go to Speak-Up-Sayeh's house, where everyone speaks quietly?

'Mrs Brisbane, who is taking Humphrey home?' Heidi Hopper asked.

'Raise-Your-Hand-Heidi,' Mrs Brisbane told her.

Heidi forgets to raise her hand sometimes.

'I am!' Mandy Payne said. She forgot to raise her hand, too!

'That clock must be stuck. It's taking forever to get to the end of the day,' Mandy complained.

Don't-Complain-Mandy-Payne used to complain about a lot of things.

But since she got her own hamster, Winky, she doesn't complain as much.

'I can't wait!' I shouted.

My friends giggled, even though all they heard me say was 'SQUEAK-SQUEAK-SQUEAK!'

Just then, the clock hand moved and the bell rang.

The end of the day had finally come!

My friend Og splashed loudly in his tank.

He's a classroom pet, too, but he

doesn't go home with students at the weekend, because he doesn't have to be fed every day, like I do.

'I'll tell you all about my weekend at Mandy's when I get back,' I squeaked.

'BOING-BOING-BOING!' he replied, hopping up and down.

He makes a funny sound because he's a funny frog.

Soon Mandy's mum arrived to pick us up.

'Humphwee!' a tiny voice shouted.

It was Mandy's little brother.

'Hi, Bwian,' I squeaked back.

His name is 'Brian', but he calls himself 'Bwian'.

Mandy's younger sisters, Pammy and Tammy, rushed up to my cage.

'*I'm* going to take care of you, Humphrey,' Pammy said.

'No, *I'm* going to take care of you, Humphrey,' Tammy said.

The girls are twins, but they don't look at all alike.

'*I'm* going to take care of Humphrey, because he's *my* classroom pet,' Mandy said.

It wasn't easy, but soon Mrs Payne had all four children, my cage, my food and me in the car.

It took *forever* to get to the Paynes' house.

Then, Mrs Payne had to get all four children, my cage, my food and me into the house.

That took even *longer*.

But at last, my cage was on a table in the living room, right next to Winky's cage!

'Hi, Humphrey!' Winky said.

When Winky was born, one of his eyes didn't open, so he always looks like he's winking.

'Hi, Winky!' I replied. 'How are things going?'

'Everything is hamster-iffic with me,' he squeaked.

'Same with me,' I said.

Winky is the only one I know who can understand my squeaks, because he's a hamster, too.

'Glad you could visit, Humph,' Winky said. 'Wait until you see my wheels.'

I looked closely at Winky.

He had four paws, just like me, but I didn't see any wheels.

'What wheels?' I asked.

'My car,' he said. 'The Paynes got me my very own car.'

I had a lovely, big cage, a wheel for spinning, a mirror, a little bell, and a hamster ball.

But I *didn't* have a car.

'Look at them. They're talking,' Mandy squealed.

Tammy, Pammy and Bwian — I mean Brian — all giggled.

'What are they talking about?' Mandy said. 'Oh, I know! Humphrey wants to see Winky's car!'

Before I knew what was happening, Mandy took Winky out of his cage and put him into a hamster-sized car.

It was bright blue and it had four wheels.

In the middle was a bigger wheel, like the wheel I spin on.

This was one really wheely car!

'It's unsqueakably wonderful!' I said.

'Watch this!' Mandy put Winky
in the big wheel and he started
spinning.

As the wheel spun, the car began
to roll.

Mandy took me out of my cage
and held me in her hand so I could
watch.

'Go, Winky!' I squeaked.

'Go, Winky, go!' Pammy, Tammy and Brian shouted.

Winky made the wheel go faster and faster.

Zoom! The car glided across the room.

Mandy picked the car up and turned it around.

Zoom! The car glided across the room in the other direction.

'Go, Winky, go!' Mandy shouted.

I think I have a wonderful life as the classroom pet in Room 26.

I think it's the best life a hamster ever had.

But I have to admit, I was a TINY-TINY-TINY bit jealous of Winky.

I wanted a really wheely car, too!

After a while, Mandy stopped the car and took Winky out.

'I don't want you to get tired,' she said as she put him back in the cage.

'Thanks, Mandy!' he squeaked.

Of course, I was the only one who could understand him.

'Do you mind sharing?' she asked Winky.

Winky squeaked. 'Not at all.'

Before I knew what was happening, Mandy put *me* in the car.

The car felt a lot like my nice yellow hamster ball.

But this was no everyday hamster ball. This was a really wheely car!

I started spinning on the wheel. Zoom! The car lurched forward.

Zoom! I spun faster and the car rolled across the room.

I spun faster and faster. Zoom! Zoom!

'Go, Humphrey, go!' Mandy shouted.

'Go, go, go,' Pammy, Tammy and Brian shouted.

I was going a little too fast, and the car slammed into the wall.

Zoom! The car spun around and rolled in the other direction.

'Isn't it fun?' Winky squeaked.

'It's the most fun I've ever had,' I shouted.

ZOOM-ZOOM-ZOOM!

I could have spun that wheel forever.

For the rest of the weekend, Winky and I took turns racing the bright blue car.

Sometimes Mandy put me in my hamster ball, so Winky and I could roll along next to each other.

It was fun, but my hamster ball doesn't have wheels.

'If you had a car, we could have a *real* race,' Winky said.

'I hope I'll have a really wheely car of my own some day,' I told Winky on Sunday night.

'I hope so, too, Humphrey,' Winky said with a wink. 'I really do.'

ZOOM-ZOOM-ZOOM Around the Room

'Og, there was a car and it was blue and I went ZOOM-ZOOM-ZOOM ...' I squeaked to my neighbour when I got back to Room 26 on Monday.

'BOING-BOING-BOING-BOING!' Og jumped up and down in his tank.

'I'll tell you the rest later,' I said.

The bell rang and class began. Before our maths lesson, Mrs Brisbane asked Mandy to tell the class about our weekend.

'It was great,' Mandy said. 'I think Humphrey and Winky were happy to see each other. At least they squeaked a lot.'

My friends giggled. Stop-Giggling-Gail laughed the loudest.

'And Humphrey really loved rolling around in Winky's hamster car,' Mandy explained.

'Car?' AJ said in his loud voice. 'He has a *car*?'

Mandy nodded. 'Yes. It's like a hamster wheel, but it looks like a car. Humphrey loved it as much as Winky does.'

'I've never seen a hamster car,' Pay-Attention-Art said.

'Me neither,' Heidi added.

'Well . . . I brought it with me,' Mandy said. 'Is it all right to show them, Mrs Brisbane?'

Mrs Brisbane smiled. 'Of course, Mandy. I'd like to see it, too.'

Mandy reached in her rucksack
and there it was. The little blue car!

'Oooh,' my classmates
said.

'Ahhh,' Mrs Brisbane said. 'Why
don't you show us how it works?'

Mandy gently took me out of my
cage and put me in the racing car.

She set the car on the floor and I began to spin the wheel.

'Go, Humphrey, go!' Richie shouted as I rolled the car between the students' tables.

I spun the wheel a little faster.

'Faster, Humphrey, faster!' I heard AJ shout.

'BOING-BOING-BOING!' Og yelled as he splashed in the water side of his tank.

My friends all stood up to watch me, so I spun even faster.

I had a difficult time rounding the corner near Wait-for-the-Bell-Garth's foot, but I managed to keep going.

'I hope he doesn't lose control,' Mrs Brisbane said.

It wasn't easy, but I kept the car going without rolling *into* something.

'Humphrey! Humphrey! Humphrey!' my classmates chanted.

All their cheering made me spin even faster.

I spun so hard, I felt DIZZY-DIZZY-DIZZY.

Before I knew it, my car rolled up against the leg of Mrs Brisbane's desk.

The car bounced off the leg and spun even faster until it suddenly stopped . . . like THAT!

Mrs Brisbane had stopped the car with her foot.

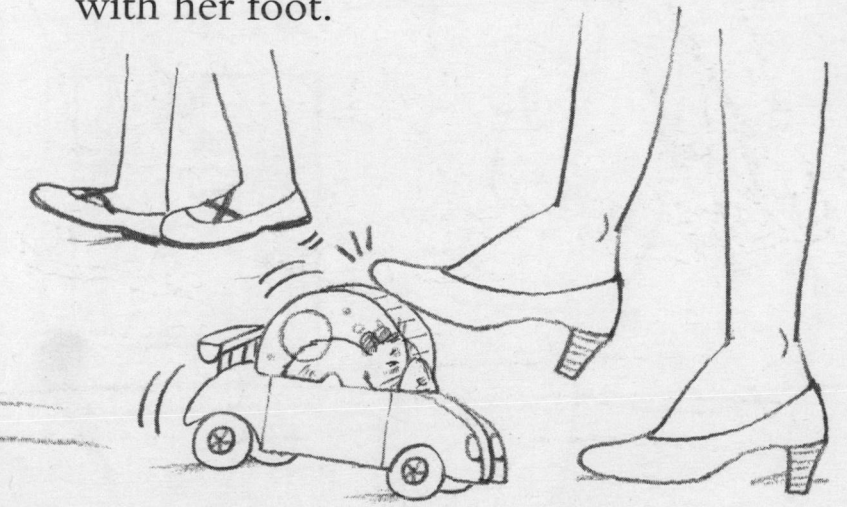

'Humphrey, I think you need a rest,' she said.

I had to admit she was right.

'I can see that Humphrey had a great time at your house,' Mrs Brisbane told Mandy, as she put me in my cage.

'Yes,' Mandy replied. 'I put Humphrey in his hamster ball and Winky in the car and they raced each other,' she said. 'But I think Humphrey would like his own car. Then they could have a *real* race.'

'A hamster race!' Garth said. 'I'd like to see that!'

'Humphrey should have his own car,' Golden-Miranda said.

'That's right!' AJ said in his LOUD-LOUD-LOUD voice. 'They could race, and I know Humphrey-Dumpty would win!'

I like the funny nickname AJ made up for me.

'Thanks!' I squeaked.

'BOING-BOING!' Og said.

When I looked around, all my classmates were smiling.

'Winky might win. He knows how to make his car go really fast,' Mandy said. 'But the car costs a lot of money. The only way I got Winky's car was by asking for it for my birthday.'

Money! Sometimes I forget about human things, like money.

My friends weren't smiling any more.

'We'll find a way. Let me think about it,' Mrs Brisbane said. 'Now, it's time to start our maths.'

It wasn't easy for me to think

about maths after all that
excitement.

When Mrs Brisbane wrote
an '8' on the board, it looked
like a race track with fun
twists and turns.

Later, while my friends studied science, Mrs Brisbane put me in the car and let me roll around Room 26.

It was fun, but not as much fun as being in my own car and racing Winky would be.

Even worse, at the end of the day, Mrs Brisbane gave the car back to Mandy.

'I'm sure Winky will want this,' she said.

'Yes,' Mandy said. 'But I hope Humphrey gets a car, too.'

'YES-YES-YES!' I squeaked.

'BOING-BOING-BOING!' Og took a big leap into the water side of his tank.

Mandy giggled. 'I forgot about Og. I wonder if they have frog cars.'

'Now that would be funny!' Mrs Brisbane said with a smile.

★

That evening, when Og and I were alone, I opened the lock-that-doesn't-lock on my cage and walked over to Og's tank.

'Do you want to be in a race?' I asked.

'BOING.' Og didn't sound very sure.

'Well, I do,' I said. 'And if there's a car for hamsters, there should be a car for frogs, too.'

'BOING-BOING!' Og seemed more interested.

I tried to picture Og driving a car.

With his big webbed feet, I didn't see how he could spin the wheel to make it go.

'Don't be upset,' I told him. 'I don't have a car, either.'

Og and I were quiet for the rest of the evening.

At least I could imagine having a really wheely car, even if it wasn't the same at all.

Really Wheely and Red

The next morning, Mrs Brisbane entered Room 26 with a big smile on her face and a large box in her hand. She said, 'Last night, I went to Pet-O-Rama.'

Pet-O-Rama? That's the pet shop where I used to live!

'I told the manager we want to have a hamster car race,' Mrs

Brisbane explained. 'And he wants to help us.'

The manager – my old friend Carl – wanted to help?

'YIPPEE-YIPPEE-YIPPEE!' I squeaked.

My friends looked as happy as I was.

The door opened and Mr Morales, the head of Longfellow School, walked in.

'Good morning, class,' he said.

He turned to Mrs Brisbane. 'What did you want to show me?'

'This,' our teacher said.

She picked up the box and opened the lid.

Then she reached in and took out a car.

It wasn't a real car.

It was a really wheely hamster car!

And it was bright red with flames painted on the side!

'Eeek!' I squeaked. 'It's just what I wanted.'

Mrs Brisbane told Mr Morales about Winky's car and the idea about a hamster race.

'Pet-O-Rama is giving this car to Humphrey,' she said.

I was so surprised, my whiskers wiggled and my tail twitched.

'It has the pet shop name on the back,' she said.

I scrambled to the tippy-top of my cage to get a better look.

It was true. 'Pet-O-Rama' was written on the back of the red racing car.

'Pet-O-Rama will also donate prizes for the winner,' she said.

I LIKED-LIKED-LIKED that idea!

'I'd like to see a hamster race myself,' Mr Morales said.

'BOING!' my neighbour agreed.

'Og!' Mr Morales said. 'What do you think of a hamster race?'

Og bounced up and down in his tank.

'BOING-BOING-BOING!' he said.

'We should have a frog race, too,'

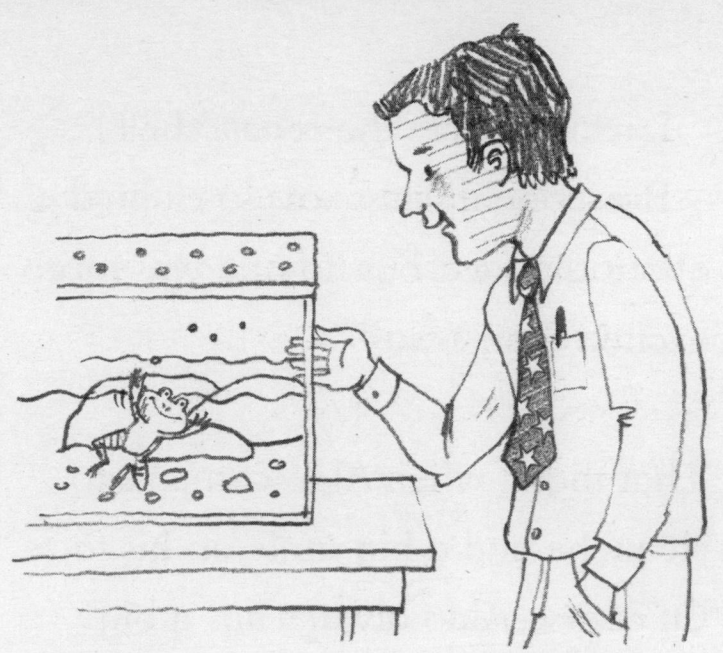

Mr Morales said. 'But I don't think they have cars for frogs.'

'Sorry, Og,' I squeaked to my friend.

'We'll make our plans tomorrow,' Mrs Brisbane said. 'Time to put this away.'

She took the red car and put it on a bookcase shelf.

Luckily, it was the *bottom* shelf!

Everyone in class was so excited about the race, but no one was more excited than I was!

★

That night, when Aldo came in to clean, he had a big smile on his face. Of course, Aldo always has a big smile each night he comes to Room 26.

'Humphrey! I heard the news,' he said as he pushed his cleaning trolley through the door.

'I hear there's going to be a racing day,' he said.

'BOING-BOING,' Og chimed in.

Aldo began to sweep the floor.

'That's one race I'm not going
to miss,' he said. 'After all, I have to
cheer for my buddy.'

'Thanks, Aldo!' I squeaked.

I LOVE-LOVE-LOVE it when
Aldo comes to clean.

But I have to admit, I was happy
when he left that night.

As soon as he was gone,
I jiggled the lock-that-
doesn't-lock on my cage.

The door opened wide
and I scurried across the
table.

'I'm going for a ride,
Og,' I squeaked.

I slid down the leg of
the table and ran across
the floor to the bookcase.

There it was. The bright shiny red car!

I pulled myself up on to the bottom shelf of the bookcase.

I wanted to take it for a spin, so I gave it a little push.

The car rolled off the shelf and hit the floor with a BUMP.

It ROLLED-ROLLED-ROLLED across the floor.

'Wait for me!' I shouted.

The car rolled between the tables in Room 26.

'Stop!' I squeaked.

'BOING-BOING!' Og sounded worried.

Just then, the car hit the leg of AJ's chair and it stopped.

'Thank you,' I said.

I stood up on my tippy-toes and popped the side door open.

Then I climbed inside.

'Here goes, Og!' I squeaked.

I began to spin the wheel.

The car started slowly.

Then I spun the wheel faster. And faster.

The car zoomed across the room.

'BOING-BOING-BOING!' Og cheered.

I thought about Winky racing next to me in his blue car, so I spun even faster.

Then I remembered that my car didn't have a steering wheel, so I couldn't turn it.

'Eeek!' I squeaked.

I stopped spinning, but the car kept on going until – BUMP! It hit the wall and stopped.

I climbed out of the top, which I hadn't been able to close with my paws.

'BOING-BOING-BOING!' Og leaped up really high!

'I'm fine, Og,' I told him. 'But I don't think I can drive the car out of the corner.'

'BOING!' Og dived into the water side of his tank and started splashing.

I have to admit, I was WORRIED-WORRIED-WORRIED. Wouldn't Mrs Brisbane wonder how the car ended up in the corner?

Or what if she couldn't find it the next morning? Would she call off the race?

What if she found out that I had a lock-that-doesn't-lock ... and then fixed it?

I could never get out and have an adventure again!

Then I had an unsqueakably good idea.

I squeezed into the corner and began to *push* the car towards the room.

UMPH! I'm a very strong hamster, but it was much harder to move the car that way.

I pushed for a while.

Then I rested for a while.

I pushed and rested for the rest of
the night.

There was sunlight peeking
through the window when I finally
got the car to the bookcase.

Of course, I couldn't push it up on
the shelf, but at least Mrs Brisbane
would see it there.

I scurried across the floor and used the cord from the blinds to swing myself back on to the table, as I've done so many times before.

'I did it,' I squeaked as I raced past Og's tank. 'BOING-BOING!' Og said.

I pulled the cage door behind me and went into my sleeping hut.

I was so tired, I slept through maths, reading *and* science.

After all, I'd had a LONG-LONG-LONG night.

I was unsqueakably surprised when I woke up and heard Mrs Brisbane say, 'Class, the great hamster race will be this Friday.'

'Eeek!' I squeaked.

'That's right, Humphrey,' Mrs Brisbane said. 'You'd better practise.'

She went over to the bookcase to get my really wheely car.

'What's it doing on the floor?' she asked. 'Maybe it rolled out when Aldo was cleaning last night.'

'Yes!' I squeaked.

It was a fib, but at least my lock-that-doesn't-lock was safe!

A Wheely Big Day

For the next few days, Mrs Brisbane let me practise racing my car around Room 26 while my friends took spelling tests and solved maths problems.

One afternoon, they made little banners on sticks.

'We'll all be sure to wave our banners to cheer Humphrey and

Winky on,' Mrs Brisbane explained.

'I let Winky ride his car every night,' Mandy said.

'Good,' I squeaked. 'May the best hamster win.'

As soon as I said it, I realised that in the end, Winky might end up winning.

But at least I'd give the race my *best*.

★

Friday was a very surprising day!

First, Mandy arrived at school with Winky.

She put his cage on the table by the window next to mine.

Winky had never been to school before.

After sitting through the morning lessons, Winky told Og and me that he thought being a classroom pet was unsqueakably wonderful.

'But I still love being Mandy's hamster,' he said.

Of course he did!

After lunch, Mrs Brisbane announced that the race was about to begin.

The whole class lined up and went out into the big hallway.

Mandy carried Winky's cage.

Miranda carried my cage.

'What about Og? He'll feel left out,' AJ said.

'No, he won't,' Mrs Brisbane said. 'I have a surprise for Og.'

A surprise for Og? What could it be?

Some of the other classes from

Longfellow school were already lined up on both sides of the hallway.

Down the middle, there were racing lanes divided by rows of wooden blocks.

There were two lines taped to the floor.

One line was marked 'Start.'

The other line was marked 'Finish.'

Mr Morales stood by the line marked 'Start.'

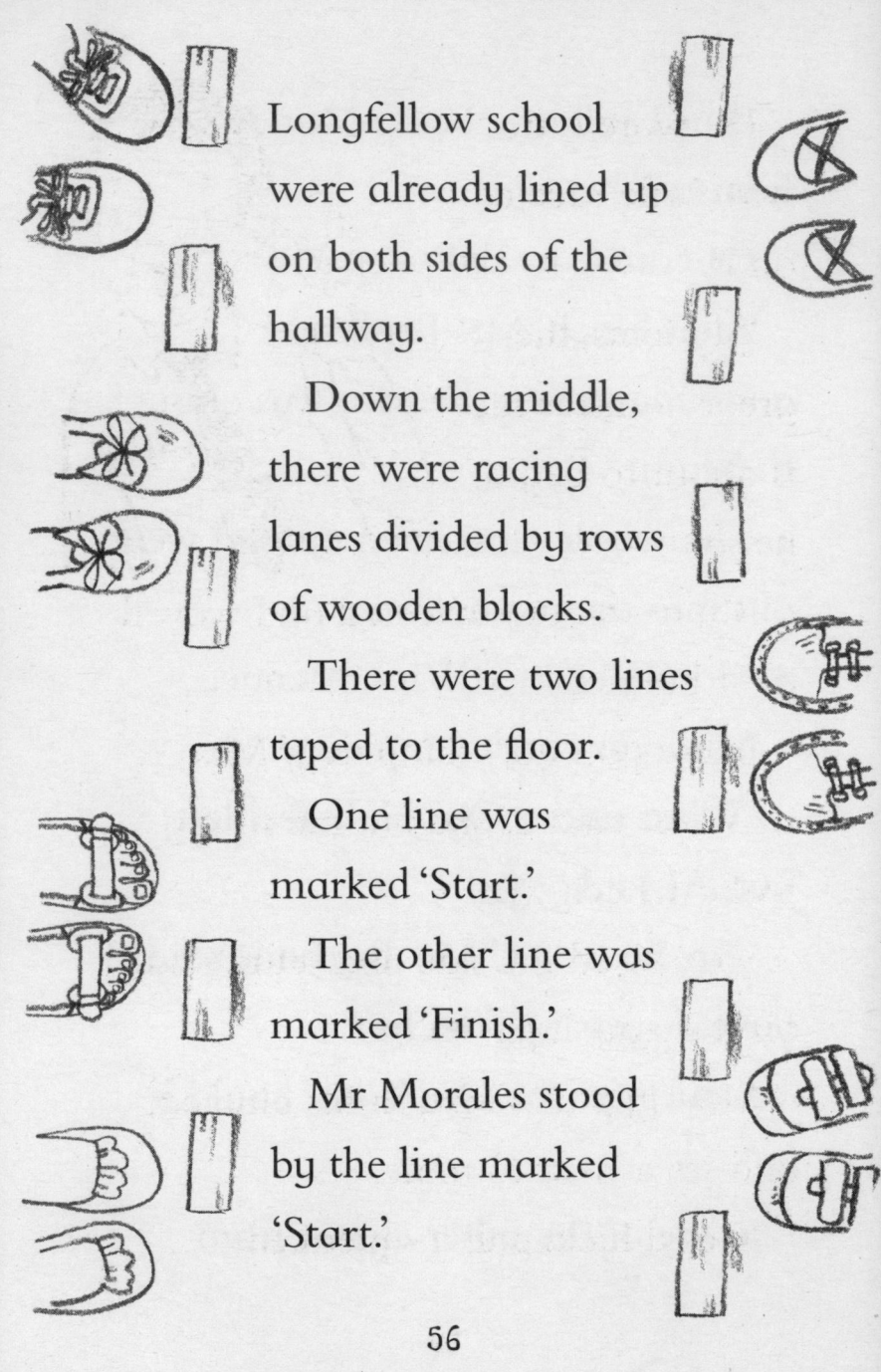

He wore a tie
with little race cars
on it.

'Students, the
great hamster race
is about to begin,'
he said.

My classmates cheered and waved
their banners.

'Here you go, Humphrey,' Mrs
Brisbane said as she put me in my
really wheely car.

She closed the side and set the car
on the start line.

Mandy put Winky in his blue car
and set it next to mine.

'Good luck, pal!' I squeaked.

'Same to you, Humph!' Winky replied.

Mr Morales said, 'Ready, steady, go!'

Mrs Brisbane gave my car a gentle push.

I didn't waste any time in getting the wheel spinning.

I kept my eyes straight ahead as I spun faster and faster.

'Humphrey, you're ahead!' the students chanted.

'Faster, Winky! You can win!' they cheered.

I looked back.

Yes, I was ahead, but Winky was close behind me.

I spun my wheel even faster.

And then a terrible thing
happened.

I was spinning as fast as I could,
but my really wheely car wasn't
moving!

It had rolled up against a wooden
block.

I was stuck!

I heard people moaning. 'Oh, no,
Humphrey!'

I heard the crowd shout, 'Go,
Winky! There's the finish line!'

Winky was going to win.

I spun and spun but the car didn't
budge, so I did the only thing I could.

I reached over and pushed the side
door of the car as hard as I could.

Success! The door opened and I
crawled out of the car.

Maybe I couldn't win the race in
my car, but I could still cross the line
first!

The cheering got louder and
louder.

As I raced for the finish line, I saw
the banners waving above me.

I glanced up over the wooden
blocks and saw Winky's blue car just

inches ahead of me.

I ran and ran as fast as my paws could carry me and I passed the blue car!

The finish line was right in front of me, so I sprinted across it.

Winky's blue car crossed the line a
few seconds later.

I had won!

Or so I thought.

'Humphrey! Humphrey!
Humphrey!' the crowd cheered.

Mrs Brisbane scooped me up and
held me in her hand.

'Quiet, everyone!' Mr Morales said.

Since he is the Most Important
Person at Longfellow School, the
crowd quietened down.

'Humphrey crossed the finish line
first,' he said. 'But he wasn't in his
car. This was a hamster car race, so I
think Winky is the winner.'

'No!' I heard some students say.

'Winky was the first hamster to cross the line in his car,' he said.

'But Humphrey was so smart,' Golden–Miranda said. 'He knew he was stuck and he still found a way to win.'

Mr Morales nodded. 'That's true,' he said. 'And I'm proud of Humphrey. But I still think that Winky won.'

'I have an idea,' another voice said.

I knew that voice.

Aldo stepped forward.

'What if we call it a tie?' he asked.

Mr Morales thought. 'We could do that,' he said.

Suddenly everyone began to cheer.

'Tie! Tie! Tie!'

Mr Morales raised both hands to quieten them down.

'All right,' he said. 'I think we can call this a tie. Is that all right with you, Mandy?'

'They both did a great job,' Mandy said. 'Winky is my pet and Humphrey is my classroom's pet. So I think . . . it's a tie!'

The cheering was so loud, it hurt my small hamster ears.

'Humphrey and Winky will each receive a First Place certificate *and* a box of Hamster Chew-Chews from Pet-O-Rama,' Mr Morales said.

I LOVE-LOVE-LOVE Hamster Chew-Chews.

The crowd got noisy again, but Mr Morales raised his hands.

'We have one more contest this afternoon,' he said. 'Longfellow School has two classroom frogs, so we're going to have a frog-jumping contest.

'BOING-BOING-BOING!' I heard Og say.

The crowd cheered.

'George is the classroom pet in Miss Loomis's class,' he said. 'Og is the pet in Mrs Brisbane's class. We're going to place them each at the starting line and see which one can jump the furthest.'

I remembered George! He was the reason that Og came to Room 26 in the first place.

Og was in Miss Loomis's class along with George, but George didn't like Og.

Since George was a huge bullfrog with a BIG-BIG-BIG voice, he made so much noise that Miss Loomis couldn't teach her class.

She gave Og to Room 26 and he's been here ever since.

'BOING-BOING-BOING!' Og shouted.

I could tell he was ready for the frog-jumping contest.

Miss Loomis set George down on the starting line.

Mrs Brisbane set Og down in his lane.

Og had a nice smile on his face.

George had a mean leer on his face.

And he was HUGE.

Could Og jump further than a great big bullfrog?

Mr Morales said, 'Ready, steady, jump!'

Miss Loomis let go of George and Mrs Brisbane let go of Og.

Nothing happened at first.

George sat on the starting line and so did Og.

Suddenly, George took a giant leap forward.

The crowd cheered, but Og didn't budge.

'Go on, Og! You can win,' I squeaked.

Og still didn't move.

'Go, Og, go!' the students chanted.

I was WORRIED-WORRIED-

WORRIED until suddenly, George let out an unsqueakably loud noise.

'RUM-RUM-RUM!' he bellowed in his deep, loud voice.

And then Og did it!

He took a huge leap forward.

He leaped past George.

Then he leaped again. And again!

'OG-OG-OG!' the crowd cheered

'Yay, Og!' I squeaked. 'I knew you could do it.'

I wasn't sure he heard me until
I heard him answer, 'BOING-
BOING-BOING-BOING!'

'The winner is Og,' Mr Morales
said. 'He will receive a jar of Froggy

Fish Sticks from
Pet-O-Rama.'

Luckily, George
didn't argue.

'BOING-
BOING-BOING!'
Og twanged.

'I want to
thank you all for our very first
Racing Day,' Mr Morales said. 'I
think Longfellow School has the best
classroom pets in the world.'

'Yes!' I squeaked.

Winky and Og were GREAT-GREAT-GREAT pets.

I tried hard to be a great pet, too.

I'm not so sure about George.

★

At the end of the day, Mrs Brisbane made an announcement.

'This week, I haven't assigned a student to take Humphrey home for the weekend,' she said.

'Eeek!' I squeaked.

After all, I love going home with students at the weekend.

'Instead, I'm taking Humphrey and Og home with *me*,' she said. 'They deserve a good rest.'

I love going home with Mrs
Brisbane.

I love it when Og can come, too.

The day had been full of surprises,
but this was the best one of all.

'Doesn't that sound like fun, Og?' I
squeaked to my friend.

'BOING-BOING-BOING-
BOING-BOING!' he replied.

I knew exactly what he meant.

Have you read all my tiny tales?

See what unsqueakably exciting adventures I've had . . .

Humphrey's Tiny Tales

My Treasure Hunt TROUBLE!

BETTY G. BIRNEY

Humphrey's Tiny Tales

My Pet Show PANIC!

BETTY G. BIRNEY

Humphrey's Tiny Tales

My Creepy-Crawly Camping ADVENTURE!

BETTY G. BIRNEY

Humphrey's Tiny Tales

My Playful Puppy PROBLEM!

BETTY G. BIRNEY

Humphrey and his friends have been hard at work making a brand new FUN-FUN-FUN website just for you!

Play Humphrey's exciting new game, share your pet pictures, find fun crafts and activities, read Humphrey's very own diary and discover all the latest news from your favourite furry friend at:

www.funwithhumphrey.com